Spell Sisters

WITH SPECIAL THANKS TO LINDA CHAPMAN

First published in Great Britain in 2013 by Simon and Schuster UK Ltd
A CBS COMPANY

Text Copyright © Hothouse Fiction Limited 2013
Illustrations copyright © Mary Hall 2013
Designed by Amy Cooper

1 3 5 7 9 10 8 6 4 2

Simon & Schuster UK Ltd
1st Floor, 222 Gray's Inn Road
London
WC1X 8HB

Simon & Schuster Australia, Sydney

Simon & Schuster India, New Delhi

A CIP catalogue record for this book is available from the British Library.

PB ISBN: 978-0-85707-253-5
eBook ISBN: 978-0-85707-696-0

Printed and bound by CPI Group (UK) Ltd, Croydon, CR0 4YY
www.simonandschuster.co.uk
www.simonandschuster.com.au
www.spellsisters.co.uk

AMBER CASTLE

Spell Sisters

OLIVIA
THE OTTER SISTER

Illustrations by Mary Hall

SIMON & SCHUSTER

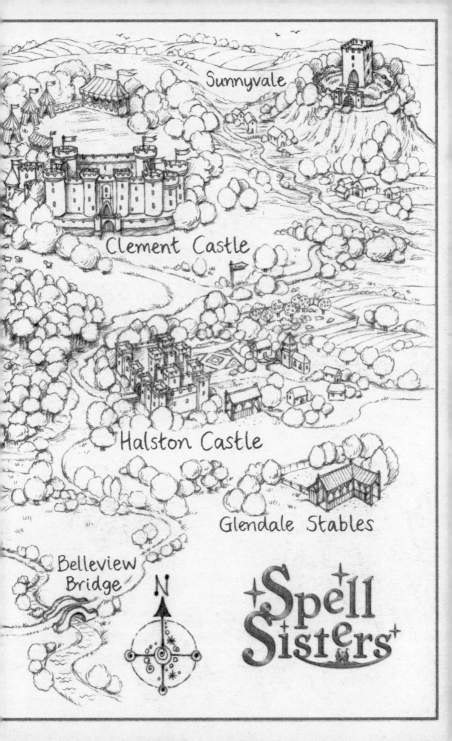

Spell Sisters

The Sun Rises...

Morgana Le Fay stood on a stone bridge, watching as the early spring sun rose in the sky, its bright rays chasing away the curtain of mist that was draped over the land. Morgana's jet-black eyes glittered.

'So, those girls defeated me yet again,' she muttered angrily. 'Well, they will never rescue the last two Spell Sisters of Avalon. I still have powers to use!' She clicked her long pale fingers. 'Come, my beauties!' she hissed. 'I command you. Come to me!'

For a moment there was no movement at all, and then suddenly, one after another, an army of rats scuttled up the bank. Their tails were long and bare, their whiskers twitched at the end of their pointed noses and their dark eyes gleamed. They surrounded Morgana.

'Oh, yes,' Morgana breathed, looking down at the moving, squeaking carpet of black fur, 'I still have power. You will help guard my prisoner, little ones. If those girls dare to come here, they will be sorry.' She stamped one foot angrily and the rats cowered. 'The lunar eclipse is not far away at all now. Soon – so *very* soon – the island of Avalon shall be mine!' Morgana laughed harshly. 'From now on, those girls will not stop me,' she snarled to the rats. 'They will *suffer* if they even try!'

A Lesson in the Sunshine

'*Grrr... rrrrr... grrrr!*'

The fluffy white puppy crouched under the table that had been moved out on to the lawn, and he snarled as Gwen tried to coax him out. It was a beautiful, unusually warm, early spring day, but the little puppy was obviously not enjoying the sunshine the way everyone else was.

'Come on now,' Gwen soothed. 'No one's

going to hurt you.'

The dog responded with another volley of suspicious yaps. Gwen frowned. Dogs usually liked her. Why was Aunt Matilda's new dog, Louis, being so unfriendly?

'Do be careful, Guinevere,' Aunt Matilda said anxiously. 'I'm not entirely sure he's safe.'

The girls were supposed to be starting some lessons out in the gardens with Gwen's aunt, but the dog had been such a distraction that they hadn't even started yet – not that it bothered Gwen too much. The longer they could hold off Aunt Matilda's lessons, the better.

Gwen held out her hand. 'Come on! Don't be so silly, boy.'

Louis lunged at her hand, teeth bared. Gwen snatched her hand back just in time and the puppy barked fiercely at her again.

Aunt Matilda patted her coiled bun, looking flushed. 'Oh dear. I know I asked for a lapdog, but why on earth did Richard get me a naughty one like *this* as a present?' She sighed. 'This dog has been misbehaving ever since he arrived here yesterday. I wanted an affectionate, friendly puppy, not a bad-tempered, aggressive one.' She shook her head disapprovingly and Gwen recognised the look straight away. It was similar to the look Aunt Matilda gave her when she did something 'unbecoming for a young lady'. She tried to hide a giggle at the thought.

'You're right, Aunt Matilda. He really doesn't seem very happy,' Gwen said, sitting back on her heels and looking at the dog. He caught her eye and snarled, his lip curling up over his teeth.

'And yet Richard said he was so sweet

and well-behaved when he saw him at the de Glanvilles' castle a few days ago.' Aunt Matilda frowned. 'I don't know what I'm going to do. I really can't bear much more of this racket.'

'Mother! Here, I've fetched him some food. Maybe this will help calm him down?' Hearing her cousin's voice, Gwen glanced round. Flora came hurrying across the castle lawn towards them, carrying a bowl containing oat biscuits and some scraps of mutton from their supper the night before. As usual, Gwen's cousin looked like the perfect example of a young noble girl. Her blonde hair was neatly tied back in two long braids trimmed with blue ribbon that matched her long dress and her big eyes. Her leather outdoor boots were polished and clean and she wore a lightweight cloak fixed with a shining brooch in the shape of a blue flower. But as she reached them, Flora tripped a little on her skirt, almost sending the food flying.

'Whoops!' she cried, recovering her balance just in time. Gwen grinned as she reached out to steady Flora. Her cousin was very lady-like, but she was also a little bit clumsy!

'Come on, Louis,' said Flora, bending down to try and tempt the dog with the bowl of food. 'Would you like a treat?' She held out a biscuit. The dog glared at her. It seemed as if even the scraps wouldn't tempt him out from under the table.

'Maybe we should just try putting it on the floor until he gets used to us,' suggested Gwen, tucking her tangle of long deep-red hair behind her ears. 'I tamed a fox cub once. To start with I just let him get used to me sitting near him while he ate and then little by little he let me get closer and touch him.'

'You tamed a fox cub!' Aunt Matilda raised her arched eyebrows. 'Dear me, Guinevere. No wonder your mother sent you here to learn how to conduct yourself. The more I hear of your childhood, the more it sounds like you were just left to run wild. Sometimes I don't know what my sister was thinking.'

Young noble girls were often sent away from their homes to live with relatives, to learn all the skills they would need when they were grown-up noblewomen. Gwen had been living at her aunt and uncle's castle for the last two years. Aunt Matilda insisted on good manners at all times and was teaching Gwen and Flora how to manage a large household full of servants as well as things like the properties of plants and flowers. She also made them practise the skills all young ladies were supposed to master such as singing, playing an instrument, painting and speaking French.

Even though Gwen loved living at the castle with Flora, who was not just her cousin but her best friend too, she found the lessons her aunt taught her very dull. She'd much rather be outside, riding, exploring the woods and shooting with her bow and arrow. She was allowed to do those things, but her aunt didn't really approve, and Flora wasn't so keen on that sort of activity. Sometimes Gwen wished she was a boy. The pages at her uncle's castle, who were the same age as her, got to go riding and practise archery as well as having races, doing gymnastics, learning to wrestle and fight with swords and joust with lances... It really wasn't fair.

Flora put the scraps on the grass and Louis started to edge closer. He gobbled the mutton up eagerly and then started to

gnaw on the hard biscuits. He certainly seemed to have a good appetite. Aunt Matilda breathed a sigh of relief. 'Well, at least we've got some quiet now. Sit back on your chairs, girls. Hopefully he will have a sleep after he's eaten. We shall carry on with your lesson on flowers and just ignore him.'

Now it was Gwen's turn to sigh. It was a pity that dealing with Louis hadn't put off their lesson for longer. Aunt Matilda looked determined to start teaching now, so she knew they had no choice. Gwen sat down obediently next to Flora. As it was such an unusually warm day for the time of year, Aunt Matilda had instructed the servants to bring a table and chairs outside into the grassy castle grounds so that she could teach the girls their lesson about flowers in the fresh air. She had put some dried flowers on the table and began to explain their properties to the girls.

'Iris flowers like this one have many uses,' she said, holding up a dried blue flower. 'They can be made into a salve to help ease toothache or painful gums, or they can be made into ink for writing with. What else. . . ? Oh, of course they have a sweet scent and can also be scattered on floors to make rooms smell pleasant. A most useful flower and I expect you both to remember the iris's many properties. I'll be checking you have been paying attention later.'

'Yes, Mother,' Flora said attentively.

Gwen quickly stifled a yawn and hoped Aunt Matilda wouldn't notice as she leaned her head against the wooden back of the heavy chair. The sun soaked into her clothes – still more suitable for winter despite the sunny weather – and she let her aunt's voice fade away in her head as she imagined everything she would rather be doing. Riding in the woods, exploring the countryside outside the castle. . .

Gwen's green eyes flew open as Flora kicked her ankle and gave her a warning look, glancing at her mother who thankfully hadn't noticed Gwen drifting off. Gwen blinked and tried to stay awake. She would get into lots of trouble if she fell asleep while her aunt was talking. But it was so warm. It was almost impossible to believe that only a few weeks before there had been a blanket of snow on the ground.

Flora glanced at Gwen again, with a slight smile now. She seemed to have an idea. 'Mother, maybe we could go and gather some more flowers?' she suggested suddenly. 'There are lots of daffodils and snowdrops by the river at the bottom of the hill. We could pick some and you could tell us all about them.'

Gwen nodded eagerly. Anything was better than sitting still.

Aunt Matilda considered Flora's suggestion. 'I suppose you could go and gather some more. You'd need your flower baskets though.'

Gwen jumped to her feet. 'I'll go and get them!'

Before her aunt changed her mind, Gwen ran into the castle. She hurried up the stone staircase all the way to the top floor where she and Flora shared a bedchamber. Despite the suddenly warm sun outside, it was still cool inside the castle. The stone walls and floors shut out the heat. Gwen picked up her and Flora's empty wicker baskets from the window sill and then she flung her leather travelling bag over one shoulder. It had useful things in it like string and a penknife. She really wanted to take her bow and quiver of feather-tipped arrows too – she always liked to be ready for anything – but she knew her Aunt Matilda wouldn't see the need for them if she was just meant to be picking flowers.

Gwen grudgingly left them in the room and made her way back outside. On the way, she felt her stomach growl hungrily and so decided to stop off in the kitchen. Maybe Hal, the castle cook, would give her some food to share with Flora. They could take a little picnic with them and eat it by the river.

It was hot in the kitchen from the roaring fire heating the big black oven. Hal was making pastry at the huge kitchen table, while John, the kitchen boy and general dogsbody, chopped turnips and carrots. Their faces were red from the heat and they were deep in discussion.

'Did you hear about one of the goats charging at Thomas the priest and knocking him over this morning?' John was saying. 'It butted him straight into a patch of mud!'

'Did it?' asked Gwen. John nodded at her. He and Hal were used to Gwen being in the kitchen and picking up all the village gossip.

Hal chuckled. 'I'd have given a gold coin to see Thomas covered in mud.' He shook his head. 'I'm blowed if I know what's wrong with the animals at the moment. The cows were butting heads with each other in the field this morning and the hunting dogs have been fighting in their kennels.'

'Aunt Matilda's new dog is being really

naughty too,' Gwen put in.

Hal huffed. 'What the devil's up with them all? It's like a spell's been cast on them.'

Gwen felt a shiver of unease. Maybe it *was* a spell. And if it was, she had a feeling she knew just who was to blame. . .

'Now, what can I be doing for you, young lady?' asked Hal, interrupting her thoughts.

Gwen forced her mind back to the moment. 'Flora and I are going down to the river. Please could we have some food to take along with us? Even if you've just got a couple of oat cakes to spare, that would be lovely.'

'I can do better than that. How about some fresh bread and cheese?' Hal fetched a couple of rolls and some cheese from the pantry. He wrapped everything up in a cloth, took two apples from the drawer where they were stored and handed the food to Gwen. 'That'll see you both through till supper,' he said with a smile.

'Thanks, Hal!' said Gwen gratefully.

She hurried on, breaking into a run as she headed out of the castle. She was out of breath by the time she reached Aunt Matilda and Flora. 'Here we are,' she panted.

Her aunt frowned. 'Really, Guinevere, there was no need to run in that unbecoming way. You are not a boy, you know.'

Of course I know that, Gwen thought. *Boys have much more fun!* But she bit the words back. She didn't want to annoy her aunt in case she was stopped from going down to the river. She saw her aunt still eyeing her disapprovingly and bowed her head. 'I'm sorry for running, Aunt Matilda,' Gwen said, as meekly as she could manage.

'Very well. Now, off you both go and gather

some flowers.' She frowned again. 'Guinevere, what have you got in your bag? It looks rather full.'

'Oh... Just a little food, Aunt Matilda.'

'Well, don't spoil your supper,' her aunt said.

'We won't,' Gwen promised, doing her best to be polite. Finally Aunt Matilda let them go and the girls set off towards the river.

As soon as they had crossed the drawbridge and were out of Aunt Matilda's sight, Gwen twirled round in delight. 'We've escaped!'

A Trip and a Fall

The hillside stretched away in front of Gwen, the grass a bright carpet of green. Two buzzards wheeled and circled in the blue sky, and at the bottom of the hill, the river sparkled in the sunshine and swathes of daffodils nodded their golden heads in the breeze. Gwen swung her empty basket around. 'No more learning about boring flowers!'

Flora laughed at her. 'It wasn't *that* boring. I thought it was quite interesting actually.'

Gwen blinked in astonishment. 'Interesting? Learning about flowers isn't interesting. It's interesting to run and climb, to learn about the woods and listen to the stories the minstrels tell. There's no excitement to be had learning about boring old flowers!' She lowered her voice. 'Not like the excitement of going to rescue the Spell Sisters!'

Flora caught her eye. 'You're right. Now that *is* exciting!'

They shared a secret smile. Unknown to anyone else, Gwen and Flora were helping to rescue the eight magical Spell Sisters from the beautiful, enchanted island of Avalon. The evil sorceress, Morgana Le Fay, had trapped the Sisters throughout the kingdom, stealing their powers because she wanted Avalon for herself. So far, Gwen and Flora had managed to free six of the Sisters who were now back on the island, but two more were still trapped. They had to be rescued by the time of the next lunar eclipse, or Morgana would be able to take Avalon as her own.

'It's been a long time since Nineve got in contact with us,' Gwen whispered. 'Don't you think it's strange?'

Flora nodded, her brow creasing a little. 'I do hope she's all right.'

Nineve, the Lady of the Lake, was another sorceress like Morgana, but she used her powers for good. She lived in the Lake that surrounded the island of Avalon, and had asked Gwen and Flora to help her free the Spell Sisters. She could use her magic to find out where the Sisters were trapped, but she could not leave the Lake. If she did, her magical protection spell would be broken and Morgana would be able to cross the water and get to Avalon.

Nineve had promised Gwen and Flora that she would try and find out where the last two Sisters were imprisoned, but that had been more than a month ago. They had wanted to go to the Lake for several weeks now, but it had snowed heavily and they had not been allowed out into the forest until the snow melted. Thankfully, a few days ago, the sun had come out and started blazing down. The world had seemed to turn from midwinter to spring in the blink of an eye. It was very strange to have such an abrupt change in the weather, but at least it meant that they might have a chance to get to the Lake.

It could be Morgana's doing, Gwen realised.

The animals at the castle were behaving strangely and so was the weather. Could it be because Morgana was using the powers she had stolen from the two Spell Sisters who were still trapped?

Gwen felt a sudden urgency rise up inside her. 'Flora, why don't we go to the Lake *now*? While Aunt Matilda thinks we're gathering flowers?'

'But what if Mother comes to find us? Flora said.

'She won't. She's bound to have other things to do than worry about where we are,' said Gwen.

'We can gather some flowers quickly and then go to see Nineve. As long as we're back before dinner, there won't be any problem. Come on!'

She grabbed her cousin's hand and started to run down the hill. 'Slow down!' Flora gasped, but she had no choice but to run with Gwen. She shrieked as they flew down the hill getting faster and faster. Suddenly Flora's boots caught in a rabbit hole and she tumbled over, pulling Gwen with her. They were going so fast that they both rolled over several times, only just stopping before they reached the riverbank.

Gwen sat up laughing, her chestnut hair decorated with grass. 'Whoops! That was fun!'

'Fun? Look at my clothes!' Flora wailed in alarm as she looked at the grass stains on her pale golden dress. 'What will Mother say?'

'Don't worry,' said Gwen. 'We can wash the

stains out when we get back to the castle.'

She heard laughter coming from nearby and looked round. Arthur, one of her uncle's pages, was in a small boat floating on the river. He had clearly seen what had happened and was chuckling at the sight of them.

Gwen grinned. She liked Arthur. Some of the pages at the castle were really annoying, always telling her she shouldn't do things like ride, or shoot with a bow and arrow, or climb, but Arthur was always really nice to her.

'Are you all right?' he called, starting to row over, the sun making his blond hair gleam.

'We're fine, thanks,' Gwen called back.

'*I'm* not fine. My dress is dirty and my foot hurts,' grumbled Flora.

Arthur immediately looked worried. 'Your foot hurts, Flora? I'm sorry for laughing. I didn't realise you had hurt yourself.' He climbed out of his boat, throwing its mooring rope round a rock so that it wouldn't float off. 'Here, let me help you up. Are you badly injured?'

Flora gratefully took his hand. 'Thanks, Arthur. I think I'm OK. It's probably just a

blister. I must have got it from running so fast.'
She raised a jokey eyebrow at Gwen while Arthur
helped her up.

Gwen rolled her eyes at her cousin. She
loved Flora and they were best friends, but she
did tend to act in a very girly way whenever there
was a boy around!

Arthur turned to help Gwen up too, but she
had already jumped to her feet. 'I didn't know
you had a boat, Arthur.' She went over to look
at the neat little rowing boat. It seemed very well
cared for.

'It only arrived yesterday – it's a present
from my father.' Arthur looked proudly at his
boat. 'I could take you both for a row in it if
you like.'

'How about *I* row *you* in it?' Gwen met his
gaze, a slight challenge in her eyes. Arthur was

twelve and she was eleven, but she was tall for her age and her eyes were almost level with his.

Arthur grinned. 'All right. You can row me if you want. Knowing you, you're probably better than me anyway!'

'Gwen is really good at rowing,' put in Flora with a smile, looking between the two of them. She grew up by the sea.'

For a moment Gwen thought wistfully

about the manor house where her parents and younger sister still lived. It was on a clifftop and the beach was only a few minutes' walk away. She really did miss it sometimes. 'I'd love to row if you really don't mind,' she said.

'Of course not,' said Arthur.

Gwen was just about to step into the boat when she remembered what she and Flora had been planning. She'd got so distracted by Arthur and the chance to go on a boat trip that she'd almost forgotten. 'Oh. Actually, maybe we shouldn't go,' she said suddenly.

'No, let's,' said Flora, guessing what Gwen was thinking. 'My foot really does hurt from the fall so I'm not going to be able to walk all the way to the Lake right now. Let's have a ride in Arthur's boat for a while and then go to the Lake later?'

'Why do you want to go to the Lake?' Arthur asked.

'Oh. . . no reason. We just thought it might be nice there in the sunshine,' Gwen said quickly. She knew that no one else must ever know about Nineve and the Spell Sisters. They couldn't even tell Arthur. 'But this is nice too. Let's go for a quick row before we collect our flowers. It'll be lovely being out on the river in the sunshine.'

The girls put their baskets into the boat and then Arthur helped Flora in. She settled herself down on the wooden seat, smoothing out her skirts. Arthur sat next to her and Gwen picked up the oars. She still thought they should go and see Nineve, but she didn't want to go without Flora, so it would have to wait a little while longer. For now, it felt wonderful to be on the water again, bobbing up and down, the breeze tickling her skin.

As Gwen plunged her oars into the water, they sent ripples out across the river. It made her think about the Lake again. She really hoped nothing bad had happened to Nineve.

I'll get there just as soon as I can, she vowed silently. I promise.

3

Under the Bridge

Gwen pulled on the oars, and the boat moved smoothly off down the river. It seemed alive with life. Two silver trout jumped into the air and dived back into the depths. A sleek otter swam in the shallows by the bank, its head only just poking out of the water. A dragonfly swooped in front of them, its green body glittering like a jewel, and two mallard ducks quacked from the reeds. Gwen even saw a black rat whisk quickly into his hole as they passed. She would have really enjoyed herself if it hadn't been for the nagging feeling that they really should go to the Lake and see Nineve.

'It's a beautiful day,' Arthur said.

'It is,' agreed Flora, as they rounded a bend in the river and began to head towards Belleview Bridge – a wide stone bridge that arched over the water. Its grey stones were mottled with yellow and white lichen. As they got closer, they saw Seth, one of the castle servants, sitting on the riverbank fishing with several long rods. He raised a hand in greeting.

'Hello, Seth!' Gwen called as she rowed towards him.

'Have you caught much today?' asked Arthur.

Seth shook his head. 'I've not caught a thing.' He held up the empty metal pail beside him. 'I don't know where all the fish have gone. There don't seem to be any.'

'How strange,' said Flora.

'We saw some trout back that way,' said Arthur, pointing behind them. 'And yesterday, when I was rowing, there seemed to be quite a lot of fish a little way on past the bridge.'

'Maybe I should move to a different spot,' said Seth, scratching his head. 'Lady Matilda wants trout for supper tomorrow night.'

Gwen used the oars to keep the boat level with Seth as they chatted and looked around. There was something niggling at her – something about this stretch of the river didn't feel quite right. What was it? Suddenly she realised. There wasn't a duck or a fish anywhere near

Belleview Bridge, not even a single insect skimming over the surface of the water. Looking towards the bridge, she felt a flicker of unease. The shadows under it looked still and dark. She'd felt the same kind of eerie silence and stillness before – and Morgana had always been at the root of it.

'Careful, Gwen,' Arthur said as the boat drifted towards the bank.

Gwen came to her senses and quickly pulled an oar towards her, straightening up the boat before it collided with the bank. 'Sorry!' she said hastily.

'Are you all right?' asked Flora.

'Yes. . . yes,' Gwen nodded. 'Just thinking about something.'

'Would you like me to take over?' offered Arthur.

Gwen hesitated and then nodded. 'Thanks.'
Maybe if Arthur rowed, she would have time to
check all around for any other signs of strangeness.

Gwen swapped places with Arthur. The
little boat bounced up and down on the water
as they did so, and Flora squeaked in alarm,
clutching on to the sides. But as they sat down,
the boat settled and Arthur started to row.

'Bye, Seth!' Flora called as they moved on.

The fisherman waved in reply.

Arthur rowed the boat towards the bridge. As they got closer, Gwen's feeling of unease deepened. The space under it looked like a dark tunnel, shadowy and with furry green moss coating the damp stones.

As they moved into the shadows, Flora shivered. 'I don't like it under here. It feels creepy.' Icy water dripped down from the underside of the bridge and dropped on Gwen's skin. She shivered too.

'Don't worry, we'll soon be out from underneath it,' said Arthur.

As they neared the other side of the bridge, Gwen caught sight of something in the stones alongside her – it looked like the faint outline of a girl, long hair spread around her, her face a mask of fear.

'Stop!' she exclaimed.

But the boat had just bobbed out into the sunshine again.

'What's the matter?' Arthur said in surprise.

Gwen opened and shut her mouth. What could she say? 'Um. . . I liked it under the bridge. Can we go back? It was so shady there, so nice to get out of this hot sun for a minute,' she gabbled.

Arthur looked as though he thought

she'd gone mad. 'You want to go back under the bridge? Well, we could, I suppose. But Flora didn't seem to like it much. . .'

'I didn't like it at all! Don't be silly, Gwen. I don't want to go back there,' Flora protested. 'It's much nicer out here in the sun. I. . .'

Gwen kicked the side of her foot where Arthur couldn't see. 'I really want to go back, just for a moment,' she said to her cousin, giving her a look full of meaning. 'It's so cool under the bridge, almost like it's under a *spell*.'

Flora's eyes widened. 'Oh!' She turned to Arthur, her tone instantly changing. 'Actually, Arthur, I think I would like to go back too. Please will you take us back into the shade for a little while longer?'

He shrugged. 'If that's where you both want to go, then of course I will.'

He rowed them back under the bridge. Gwen's eyes searched the damp stones. Yes! There it was! The outline was faint, but knowing where to look, she could definitely make out the outline of a girl.

Flora followed her gaze. 'It's a Spell Sister!' She clapped her hand over her mouth as she realised what she'd just said.

'What?' asked Arthur in confusion.

'What's that about your blister, Flora?' Gwen invented wildly. 'It's hurting you? Oh, you poor thing.'

'Um, yes,' said Flora in a strangled voice. 'It's really starting to sting.'

'I hope it feels better soon,' said Arthur with concern. 'Now, um, how long do you two want to stay under here?' he asked patiently, as an icy drip landed on his blond hair.

Gwen thought fast. She really wanted to get out the magic pendant that she always wore around her neck and use it to free the trapped Spell Sister. But she couldn't do that with Arthur there. It was very frustrating, but she knew they would have to leave and come back later without him.

'We can go back into the sun now,' she said with a small sigh. Arthur looked relieved and rowed them out from under the bridge again.

'Arthur, do you think you could take us over to the bank and let us off?' Gwen asked. She and Flora needed to come up with a plan. 'I think we'd better start gathering some flowers now, before we get in trouble with Aunt Matilda.'

'But what about Flora's blister? Will you be able to get back from here?' Arthur asked.

'I'll be fine,' Flora chipped in. 'We'll just walk slowly and enjoy the sunshine. There are some lovely bluebells over there on the bank. Mother will be so pleased if we pick some of those. Thanks for the ride, Arthur.'

'Well, if you're quite sure,' said Arthur.

He rowed over to the bank and held the boat steady for them as they got out. 'I'll head back to the castle then.'

They waved to him as he got back into the boat and rowed away under the bridge.

The second Arthur was out of earshot, the words burst out of Flora. 'There's a Spell Sister trapped under the bridge, Gwen!'

'I know! I can't believe Morgana imprisoned her so close to the castle. We've got to rescue her!' said Gwen in excitement. 'Come on!'.

'Wait a minute, Gwen!' Gwen swung round.

'I've just thought of something. What about Nineve?' Flora went on. 'We haven't heard from her. What if. . . what if this is a trick of some sort by Morgana?'

They stared at each other. Gwen felt her excitement fade. She hadn't thought about that.

'Maybe we should go to the Lake first and see Nineve,' said Flora cautiously.

Gwen hesitated. 'It'll take ages to get there.'

'I know, but we can't risk walking into a trap. There are only two Sisters left to find. Morgana's bound to be trying to stop us. She could have just made it look like there was a Sister under the bridge.'

Gwen nodded. There was a lot of sense in Flora's words, but she hated the thought of just leaving the girl trapped there. What if she was a real Spell Sister?

'Oh, if only we could speak to Nineve and find out what we should do!' she said. She pulled the pendant out from under her dress. It was a deep sparkling blue and hung on a silver chain. Next to it were six other jewels. Each of the Spell Sisters whom Gwen and Flora had rescued had added a jewel to the necklace upon their return to Avalon, as a way of thanking them. Gwen looked at the  pendant thoughtfully. 'Nineve has talked to us through the pendant before when we've been away from her. Maybe we can use it to talk to her now?'

'That's a good idea,' said Flora. 'But how do we make it work?'

'I don't know,' Gwen admitted. She tried shaking the pendant and then rubbing it, but nothing happened.

'Nineve,' she whispered to it desperately. 'Can you hear us?'

The pendant simply glinted silently in the sunlight.

Flora looked at her worriedly. 'What do we do now?'

A Message From Nineve

‘I think you're right, Flora. We'll simply have to go to the Lake to speak to Nineve.’ Gwen hesitated. ‘But then. . . ’ She paused. ‘What if it is a trapped Spell Sister? We can't just leave her here. Maybe Morgana will take that chance to move her, or even worse. . . ’ She sighed, feeling so confused about what the right thing to do was.

Flora frowned. 'Let's think about this for a moment. Can I see the pendant?'

Gwen passed it to her.

Flora examined it. 'When Nineve searches for the places where Spell Sisters might be trapped, she always uses the water in the Lake. In fact, all her magic is to do with water. . . so maybe, if we splash some water on the pendant, it will work.' Flora looked hopefully at Gwen.

'It's definitely worth a try!' Gwen scooped up a handful of water and trickled it over the pendant.

A mist swirled across its surface and suddenly they saw Nineve's beautiful face.

'You were right, Flora!' Gwen cried in delight. But as she spoke, the water dried and the image faded.

'We need more water!' said Flora.

Gwen gently lowered the pendant into the river. White mist swirled over the surface again and Nineve appeared again.

'Nineve! It's us! Gwen and Flora!'

'Girls!' Nineve's relieved voice echoed out of the pendant. Her dark eyes looked strained. 'Oh, I am so glad you have contacted me! I have been trying to reach you, but Morgana has used the power she still holds over the weather to cast a spell on the Lake. It's frozen over so that I cannot use my water magic. Look!' Her face faded to be replaced with an image of the Lake in the centre of the forest. The water had turned to ice. The girls could see Nineve's feet balancing on the frozen surface.

'Are you all right?' Gwen asked anxiously.

'Yes, I am fine. The ice stops me using some of my magic, but it cannot hurt me. I'm sure

Morgana thought it would weaken my protection spell, but still she cannot cross. However, it has meant that I have been unable to find the final two Spell Sisters or send a message to you,' Nineve said. 'The freed Sisters have been trying to help me break the weather spell, but with two of them still missing, they are not powerful enough.'

Gwen and Flora stared into the pendant, both their brows furrowed in concern.

'I am getting very worried,' Nineve continued. 'There are only a few weeks before the lunar eclipse. Time is running out.'

'Oh, but we have news, Nineve! We think we

might have found one of the Sisters,' said Gwen excitedly. She quickly explained what they had seen at the bridge. Nineve's face lit up.

'I wonder if it's Olivia the Otter Sister? Her magic is connected to animals and just before the Lake froze over I had started to see some pictures of her. She looked as if she was trapped near water and stone.'

'It could be her!' said Gwen eagerly.

'We were worried it might be a trap,' said Flora.

'You were wise to be wary,' said Nineve. 'Morgana will use the strongest magic to stop you freeing the last two Spell Sisters. But it sounds like it might indeed be Olivia.'

Gwen's eyes flashed with determination. 'If there's even the smallest chance that it is her, then we'll have to try and rescue her! If we can, we'll free her and bring her back to Avalon.'

'Oh, thank you!' Nineve said in delight. 'But be careful, both of you, please. Keep your eye out for any trouble from Morgana.'

'We will,' Flora promised.

'We'll speak to you again very soon, Nineve,' said Gwen.

'May Avalon's luck be with you,' wished Nineve.

Gwen took the pendant out of the water and the image of Nineve began to fade. 'So, it probably is a Spell Sister!' Gwen said to Flora with a grin. 'Come on, let's go!'

The two girls started to run to the bridge, but as they did so, Arthur came rowing back underneath it. 'Gwen! Flora!' he called urgently. 'Lady Matilda is looking for you. She came down from the castle to see where you'd got to.

I told her I'd come and fetch you. She didn't seem very happy that you'd been gone for so long.'

Gwen and Flora looked at each other in dismay.

'I wouldn't keep her waiting if I were you,' said Arthur, pulling the boat into the bank. 'I'll take you back.'

'We were supposed to be gathering flowers!' Flora remembered. 'Quick, Gwen. Pick some now and we can take them back with us otherwise Mother will be *really* cross.' She started grabbing daffodils, early pink campion and bluebells from the long grass around the riverbank and stuffing them into her basket.

Gwen wanted to stamp her foot. They had to rescue Olivia, but how could they with Aunt Matilda waiting for them? She gritted her teeth and pulled handfuls of flowers up too, throwing them haphazardly into her basket and then clambering into the boat. Arthur steadied it as Flora got in too and then set off, pulling the oars quickly through the water. As they passed under the bridge, Gwen looked at the faint image of the Spell Sister in the stone. She itched to pull out the pendant, press it against her and say the magic spell that would release Olivia, but there was nothing she could do about it as the boat slowly passed by the image.

'Really, girls, where did you get to?' Lady Matilda scolded, coming down to the riverbank as they got out of Arthur's boat. She looked at them sternly. 'I gave you permission to go and gather flowers, not head off in a rowing boat!'

'We're sorry, Mother.' Flora looked very apologetic. 'It was just such a lovely day we got carried away.'

Her mother caught sight of the grass stains on her dress. 'Flora! Look at your dress! You have marks all over it.'

Gwen was glad her own dress was a dark green colour and didn't show the stains.

'Sorry, Mother,' said Flora again. 'We fell over on the way down the hill.'

Aunt Matilda's frown deepened. 'Fell over? That is not very lady-like. You must be more careful.'

'We will be, Mother,' sighed Flora.

'Well, at least you picked some flowers,' Lady Matilda sniffed as she looked at their baskets. 'Though I would like to see them more carefully laid out. Now, bring your flowers inside and I shall tell you about them, and then it will be time for your French lesson.' She turned and swept away. Flora ran after her. Gwen caught Arthur giving her a sympathetic look and she grimaced at him.

As she did so, her aunt glanced round and Gwen hastily assumed a meek expression. She knew that if she displeased her aunt any more than she already had, she was in danger of being confined to the castle. She couldn't risk that, especially not now there was a Spell Sister nearby to rescue.

She followed her aunt and Flora up the hill. The three of them went into the Great Hall and Aunt Matilda made them spread the flowers they had gathered through the dried rushes that covered the floor. While they worked, she explained about the properties of campion, daffodils and bluebells.

The words buzzed around in Gwen's head like the hum of bumblebees in the castle gardens. She barely listened to a single word her aunt said. All she could think about was the Sister trapped under the bridge. Was it Olivia? When would they be able to try and rescue her? What if Morgana moved her before they could return?

After they had listened to the lecture on flowers, they had a French lesson. By now, Gwen was really starting to despair. It seemed as if they would never get a chance to escape from Aunt Matilda's lessons. Then as they were reciting a long list of French words, Louis trotted into the hall. He started to yap when he saw them all. 'Be quiet, Louis!' said Aunt Matilda. She shooed her hands at him. 'Go away!'

The dog growled at her.

'Go on!' she said firmly. 'Get out of here,
you bad dog!'

Louis didn't listen. He ran over and seized
the hem of her dress, pulling back and shaking it
as if it was a rat. Lady Matilda shrieked in alarm.
Gwen jumped off her chair and grabbed Louis

tightly by the collar. He squirmed and tried to snap at her.

'Oh my goodness,' cried Lady Matilda, fanning herself with her hand. 'That dog will be the death of me. I was hoping he would stay asleep for the afternoon.'

Gwen had a sudden idea. 'Maybe Flora and I could take him out for a walk for you before supper. If we went for a really long one, it would tire him out and then he would be bound to sleep really well tonight.'

'Oh, yes,' Flora joined in, realising Gwen's plan. 'Of course we'd love to practise more French, Mother, but we're not going to be able to even hear you if Louis continues making such a row.'

As if on cue, the small dog started to bark and yap even more loudly.

'Very well! Very well!' Lady Matilda exclaimed, putting her hands to her ears. 'I really can't stand this dreadful noise a second longer. Take him away and try and tire him out as much as you can.'

Gwen could have skipped with delight. 'Absolutely, Aunt Matilda! Do you have a lead for him?'

'No, I haven't got one yet.'

'Never mind,' said Gwen hastily. 'We'll manage.' Tucking Louis firmly under one arm and holding his muzzle closed with her other hand, she hurried to the door.

Flora followed her. 'We might be out for a while, Mother,' she said.

Lady Matilda nodded and sank down into a chair. 'That's fine. I can feel one of my headaches coming on. . .'

The girls ran down the stairs from the Great Hall and out on to the sunny castle lawn. 'Now, we can free Olivia at last!' Gwen whispered.

'We do have Louis with us though,' Flora pointed out.

'It's better than not being allowed out at all,' said Gwen, and Flora nodded.

'Do you think the Sister under the bridge really is Olivia?' asked Flora.

Gwen touched the pendant around her neck and took a deep breath. 'There's only one way to find out!'

5

Danger!

Gwen and Flora hurried out of the castle, but Louis struggled in Gwen's arms, slowing her down.

'Just a minute!' she called to Flora. Pulling off the thin leather belt she wore around her waist, she made it into a lead, tying it on to Louis' collar. 'There, that will stop you running away,' she told him. He growled as she put him on the ground.

'If we run, he'll have to run with us and won't be able to bark as much,' Gwen said to Flora.

The girls set off down the hill towards the river. Louis pulled against the lead, but Gwen held on tightly and in the end he had to run alongside her.

'I hope we do tire him out!' called Flora, following more slowly and carefully so as not to fall like last time.

'Nineve said Olivia's magic is connected to animals,' Gwen called back. 'Perhaps that's why they're all behaving so oddly at the moment. If we free her, maybe Louis will start being good.' She paused as she reached the riverbank and waited for Flora to catch up.

'First we have to free her though,' Flora reminded her cousin as she reached the bank too. 'What if Morgana tries to stop us?'

Gwen swallowed. Every time they had freed a Spell Sister, Morgana had attacked them with magic. Her heart sank as she realised she didn't even have her bow and arrows with her – they were still back at the castle. But there was no time to go back and get them. 'We'll just have to think of a way to defeat her. We always manage to, don't we?' she said, trying to sound brave. 'Come on!'

Without Arthur's boat, the girls had to run all the way along the riverbank to the bridge.

'I've got a stitch,' panted Flora when they finally arrived. She sank down on to the bank, struggling to get her breath back.

Gwen could feel sweat prickling in her hair and her heart was pounding, but she didn't want to waste any more time. She started towards the base of the bridge, but Louis began pulling back on the belt, twisting this way and that. It was clear he didn't want to go anywhere near the bridge. Gwen tried to hang on to him, but the makeshift lead slipped through her fingers. With a relieved yap, Louis sped off.

'Louis!' gasped Flora. 'Come back!'

But it was too late; the little dog had already vanished into the nearby trees.

'Gwen! What will Mother say?' exclaimed Flora.

'We'll have to deal with that later,' said Gwen

anxiously. 'We've got to try and free Olivia.'

Flora nodded. 'You're right. But how are we going to get to her without a boat?'

Gwen looked at the bridge. The river lapped against the stone and there was no walkway or bank of grass to crawl along. The Spell Sister was trapped in the middle of the tunnel. How could Gwen get close enough to touch her with the pendant?

'Flora, if you hold on to me, maybe I can reach far enough into the tunnel,' she said uncertainly. Holding on to the side of the bridge, Gwen found a firm foothold and peered into the shadowy damp. 'I think I should be able to just about reach in if you grip me tightly. I'll have to lean in quite far though. . . '

Flora came over, looking uncertain. 'What if you fall in the river?'

'I suppose that's a chance I'll just have to take,' said Gwen determinedly. She glanced at the water. It looked dark and sinister and despite the sun beating down, a coldness seemed to come from it. She really hoped she wouldn't fall in. 'Right, are you ready?' she said to Flora, pulling the necklace over her head to make sure it was free to touch the Spell Sister.

Flora grabbed Gwen round the waist and braced herself as Gwen reached into the tunnel. Gwen could just see the faint outline of the Sister in the stone. She reached out further into the shadows, but she still couldn't quite touch it.

'I'm almost there,' she gasped, stretching even further.

She touched the pendant against the stone wall, but it missed the Spell Sister and just as it brushed against the stone, a gust of wind rushed through the tunnel, swirling past and pulling at her hair. Another gust followed quickly, buffeting her.

'What's happening?' cried Flora.

The wind whipped up the water around Gwen's feet.

'It must be something to do with Morgana!' yelled Gwen. 'She still has the Sister who controls the weather trapped – she must be using her stolen power to try and stop us!'

'I can't hold on to you much longer!' shouted Flora, as the wind tossed her braids round her face and sent her cloak flying round her shoulders.

Gwen tried to take a step back towards Flora, but another gust of wind caught her and she almost lost her footing. She grabbed at the side of the bridge to stop herself falling, but as she did, she felt the pendant slip from her fingers. It disappeared into the water with a splash.

'The pendant!' she shrieked, as Flora

desperately clutched Gwen to keep her steady. The two of them watched in horror as the river swept it up and carried it away.

'Quick, Flora!' yelled Gwen. 'We can't free the Spell Sisters without it!'

She tried to leap into the water, but Flora dragged her backwards with surprising strength. 'No, Gwen! You can't go into the river!' she said, still hanging on to Gwen's arm. 'Look how fast the current is. You'll be swept away too!'

'Please, Flora! I have to try!' Gwen tried to fight her off and pull free. All she could think about was getting the pendant back. If they lost it, all hope of freeing the remaining Spell Sisters would be gone and Morgana would win! Gwen was usually stronger than Flora, but fear made her cousin hang on tightly.

'I won't let go! You're not going in there!

I mean it, if you go in there, you'll have to pull me in too!'

Gwen knew her well enough to know Flora meant it, and although she herself was a strong swimmer, she knew Flora wasn't. She stopped struggling. 'OK, but we've got to do something, Flora!' she said desperately.

Flora grabbed her hand. 'Look, I can still see the pendant in the water. Let's follow the river. The current might be less strong away from the bridge and we might be able to get the pendant out then.'

Gwen nodded. She could just see it still glinting in the rushing water too. 'Come on!' she cried.

6

A Rescue Mission

Gwen stumbled and tripped as she and Flora ran along the riverbank, trying to keep up with the pendant as it was swept away by the current. *I mustn't lose it,* she thought desperately.

As she ran, Gwen spotted Seth. He had moved his fishing rods further upstream to where there were more fish, and gave her and Flora a look of surprise as they charged past, jumping over clumps of grass and dodging round bushes. 'What's the hurry?' he called.

But neither Gwen nor Flora stopped to reply. They raced on round a bend in the river. Gwen looked at the water in despair. Where was the pendant? She couldn't see it and for a moment her heart seemed to stop. Then it appeared again, glinting blue as it was swept to the surface. It swirled on, finally tangling in a patch of long reeds growing up out of the water. The chain caught fast as the pendant bounced around in the rushing water.

Gwen skidded to a halt. The reeds were quite far out. She couldn't reach them from the bank, but at least the necklace had stopped. 'Look, Flora!' she pointed as her cousin ran up behind her.

'How are we going to get to it? We can't go into the river, it's too dangerous – the pendant is so far out in those reeds,' said Flora, looking at the fast-flowing water racing past.

Gwen stood as close to the edge of the bank as she dared. 'We need something long enough to reach it and lift it off the reeds,' she said.

'A tree branch?' suggested Flora.

'It might work, if we can find one thin and long enough,' Gwen agreed. But a quick glance around showed there were no trees nearby. 'Maybe another reed will do instead?' she said, spotting some long hollow reeds beside the river. Opening her travelling bag she took out her penknife and cut a reed. 'I'm not sure it's going to be long enough,' she said as she went to the edge of the bank and leaned out. She was right – the reed was much too short. 'We'll have to go back to the forest and find a branch,' she said with a sigh.

'Why don't you go on your own?' suggested Flora. 'You're faster than me, and I can stay and keep an eye on the necklace. If it moves, I'll follow it.'

'Good idea,' said Gwen.

'Hurry then!' urged Flora. 'But be careful. Morgana might still be trying to stop us.'

Gwen set off. Her thoughts were racing. If only she'd been able to reach Olivia with the pendant and free her, then they might all have been safe by now. Instead she was in danger of losing the necklace forever and letting down Nineve and the Spell Sisters. Oh, why had she dropped it? She raced back along the riverbank. Now she had to try and find a branch that was long and thin enough to hook up the necklace –

who knew how long that would take!

As Gwen turned the corner, she saw Seth still trying to fish while fighting against the wind. Of course! A fishing rod. Why hadn't she thought of that before?

'Seth! I need your help,' she cried, charging up to him.

'Please may I borrow one of your rods for a few minutes?'

'One of my fishing rods?' Seth echoed. 'What do you want with one of those, Miss Guinevere?'

Gwen hesitated. 'I've. . . I've dropped something in the river. A necklace. It's caught on some reeds and I think I can get it back, but I need something to hook it with.' *Oh please, please, please, say yes!* she thought.

Seth shrugged. 'Well, I don't see why not.' He handed her a rod. 'Would you like me to help you? The wind's become very strong all of a sudden.'

'That's all right,' said Gwen quickly. She didn't want Seth involved in case Morgana did come along. 'I'm sure I can get it.'

Seth nodded. He knew Gwen well.

'All right, but don't go getting into any trouble now. If you need a hand, come and get me.'

'Thank you, Seth!' cried Gwen. Carrying the rod, she ran back towards Flora. She felt a rush of relief when she saw her cousin still standing in the same place. At least the necklace hadn't been carried any further.

'A fishing rod!' Flora's face lit up as she saw what Gwen was carrying. 'That's perfect.'

Gwen eyed up the distance between the bank and the necklace. It looked like it was about the length of the rod. She wound in the line until the hook was hanging at the very end. If she could catch the necklace with the fishhook, hopefully she'd be able to pull it back towards her. She stood on the bank and edged the rod out cautiously towards the reeds.

'Careful!' squeaked Flora.

Gwen felt the wind tugging at the rod, pulling it away from the reeds. She tried to push against the force of the wind, edging the hook closer to the silver chain, but it was hard – the wind was strong and was tugging the rod in the opposite direction. Concentrating hard, she edged the hook closer and closer until it was almost touching the chain. If she could just get a little bit nearer. . . She jiggled the rod and the hook moved, but the necklace slipped a little more. Gwen caught her breath. *No! She was going to lose it again!*

She waited for the necklace to be whisked away, but it stayed balanced in the reeds.

'You can do it!' Flora told her. 'Go on, Gwen.'

Gwen moved the rod down. The hook was tantalisingly close to the chain now. *Gently*, she

told herself. She moved the rod a fraction and there it was. The hook had caught round the necklace.

'I've got it!' she exclaimed.

She lifted the rod carefully and the necklace dangled from the hook, tossing around worryingly in the wind. For a moment Gwen thought it was going to fall into the river again. She held her breath and drew the rod back as quickly as she could.

'You did it!' cried Flora. Gwen took the necklace off the hook with trembling fingers. She clutched the silver chain tightly, her heart beating like a drum.

Flora hugged her. 'Thank goodness!'

'Right. Now we can rescue Olivia!' But Gwen's triumph faded as she thought about the task that still lay ahead. She picked up the fishing rod. 'Come on, let's get this rod back to Seth and then get to the bridge as quickly as we can.'

Flora's eyes met hers. 'And let's hope Morgana doesn't have any more tricks up her sleeve!'

7

Louis Saves the Day

The girls raced back down the riverbank, returning the rod to Seth on the way. 'It's a strange old day,' he said. 'I'd get back to the castle if I were you. It looks like a storm is about to break.'

'We'll go back as soon as we can,' promised Gwen. 'We've just got one thing to do first. Thank you so much for lending us the fishing rod!'

She and Flora ran on. As they raced round the bend that led towards the bridge, Gwen tensed. She half expected to see Morgana herself standing there, but the bridge looked just as it had done before, with the wind whistling around it and the water running fast. Gwen pulled the pendant over her head and held it tightly.

'Quick, let's try and reach the Spell Sister again. This time I *won't* drop the necklace!'

They ran to the base of the bridge. Once again, Flora took hold of Gwen's waist and Gwen leaned into the damp tunnel until she could just see the outline of the Sister. She leaned further and further in, feeling Flora hanging on as tightly as she could.

'I can almost reach!' said Gwen.

Suddenly, she heard a squeaking noise.

Looking round, she yelped in alarm. Hundreds of rats with black greasy fur were scuttling out of holes and along the bank towards her and Flora. Their gleaming eyes were fixed on the girls and their teeth looked yellow and sharp.

'Rats!' shrieked Flora. She let go of Gwen, who struggled to stop herself falling into the water. Leaping back on to solid ground, the girls ran backwards together, but the rats swarmed after them, crouching down and preparing to spring.

'We have to do something!' cried Flora in terror. 'They're going to bite us!'

But her words were drowned out by the sudden sound of barking behind them. It was Louis! The little dog came rushing out of the trees towards the rats, his ears pricking. He looked fluffy and cute, but Gwen remembered that his breed had once been used as ratting dogs – and Louis clearly still had it in him to hunt rodents! He raced towards the army of rats and grabbed

the leader by its neck. Tossing it into the water, he leaped on another and shook it before pouncing on a third. The rats turned tail and fled, racing back into the safety of their holes as Louis chased them this way and that.

Gwen slowly felt her heart calm down. 'Oh my goodness. That was close. The rats must also be part of Morgana's plan to stop us rescuing Olivia.'

Flora's face was pale. 'Thank goodness for Louis.' The dog turned and looked at them, panting.

'Here, boy,' said Gwen.

But Louis growled and darted at Flora's ankles, his teeth snapping.

Flora shrieked as the dog's teeth fastened on the toe of her leather boot.

'Louis! No!' Gwen shouted, but the dog continued to bite Flora's foot. Gwen took her bag off her shoulder and swung it at him, trying to scare him away. To her relief, it worked – Louis dodged the bag and backed off warily.

Suddenly Gwen remembered the bread and cheese she'd taken earlier from the palace kitchen. Maybe that would work. She opened the bag and quickly took the cheese and rolls out. The dog smelled the food straight away and looked at Gwen eagerly.

'Yes! There you are, boy. Food. Now, go and get it!' Gwen threw the chunks of cheese and bread rolls as far as she could in four different directions. Louis raced eagerly after one of the pieces of cheese.

Flora breathed out in relief. 'Oh, well done, Gwen. That was a brilliant idea.'

'Hopefully that will keep him busy,' said Gwen.

Flora shivered. 'Those rats were horrible. I hope Morgana hasn't got anything else planned. Let's free the Spell Sister and get out of here!'

Gwen was already running back over to the base of the bridge again.

With Flora hanging on to her, and feeling it was now or never, Gwen reached out once more for the outline in the stone. She didn't want to find out what Morgana had planned next to try and stop them. With her arm stretched as far as she could, Gwen pushed the pendant against the stone outline. This time she didn't miss. Holding the pendant firmly to the stone, she gasped out the spell that Nineve had once taught her:

'Spell Sister of Avalon I now release,
Return to the island and help bring peace!'

A shiver seemed to run through the bridge. For a moment the outline glowed and then the stones in the bridge started to shift and move. Gwen edged back, her heart somersaulting in her chest. 'It's working, Flora!'

Small bits of stone began to crumble away, splashing into the fast-flowing river.

'Oh goodness!' breathed Flora. 'I wonder if it is Olivia?'

The shimmering shape of a girl pressed outwards from the bridge and suddenly she was floating out of the wall. She was wearing a golden dress that swept down to her feet and her dark wavy hair framed her face, falling almost to her ankles.

She looked around, dazed. Gwen grabbed the Spell Sister's hand and guided her to the safety of the riverbank. 'Thank you,' she stammered.

'Thank you so much for setting me free. I'm Olivia.' Her gentle brown eyes were the same deep brown as a fawn's, her pale skin smattered with freckles.

'Olivia! Nineve thought it was you!' Gwen said in delight.

'If you don't mind me asking. . . who are

you?' Olivia looked bewildered. 'And how do you know the Lady of the Lake?'

Gwen quickly explained. 'I'm Gwen – Guinevere – and this is Flora, my cousin. We've been helping Nineve rescue your sisters from Morgana's spell.' Gwen quickly explained everything that had been happening since Olivia had been trapped.

'Six of your sisters are safe on Avalon now,' added Flora.

Relief rushed across Olivia's face. 'Oh thank goodness.'

Gwen shivered. The wind was turning cold. 'We must get you back to Avalon too,' she said anxiously. 'Before Morgana tries to stop us. She created this terrible wind and that's bad enough, but I'm not sure what she'll do when she realises you're free.' But as Gwen spoke, the sky started

to darken. Dark purple clouds began to race across the sun and soon great fat drops of rain were falling from the sky.

Flora looked up at the sky anxiously as a fork of lightning seared down and thunder crashed around them. 'We have to get out of here!'

Olivia looked as alarmed as the girls did. 'Come on!' she urged. The rain was really fierce now. Olivia and Flora raced off the bank and down on to the path, but as Gwen followed, her feet slipped on the bank and she fell, her fingers desperately gripping at the slippery, oozing mud by the river.

Behind her came a strange roaring sound. *What was that?* Gwen glanced round and cried out as she saw a whirlwind of water rushing towards her down the river, overspilling the banks and sweeping up everything it came across.

Gwen tried to scramble to her feet. 'Quick, Gwen!' cried Flora, from the safety of the path.

The roar of the river was deafening as the funnel of water bore down on Gwen. She managed to get to her feet just as it hit her.

'Gwen!' she heard Flora scream as she was swept up into the icy water.

And then the water closed over her head and Gwen heard no more.

8

Drowning!

Gwen tumbled over in the huge whirl of water as it twirled her round and round. Her lungs burned from holding her breath, her eyes stung. She kicked hard, her long skirt hindering her, but she managed to reach the surface and gasped in a breath of air before she was swept round again. She could feel the current trying to pull her into the centre of the whirlpool and she fought against it with all her might.

The next second, the water funnel exploded into a wave and Gwen found herself being swept along the river away from the bridge. She tossed and tumbled like a leaf in the water, trying to grab branches and reeds as she passed to stop herself being swept away, but the current was too strong. She could see Flora running along the bank, yelling her name.

I'm going to drown. The thought raced through Gwen's brain as she felt her waterlogged dress dragging her down beneath the surface.

Suddenly over the roar of the water and Flora's shouts, she heard a strange singing. It was high and haunting and cut through the sound of everything else. Gwen managed to look back over her shoulder and saw Olivia holding her hands out in front of her, singing a spell:

> *'Swift swimming otters, please listen to me,*
> *Please help my friend, let her break free.'*

Gwen was swept onwards, but within seconds, she felt the water change. Bodies began to fill it – sleek brown bodies with chubby faces, small round ears, bright sparkling eyes and long whiskers. Otters! She felt them surrounding her, helping her fight against the current, pushing her body up in her heavy dress so she could breathe in gulps of air. Gwen still couldn't stop the current from sweeping her along, but she could use her strength to stay on the surface. 'Thank you!' she gasped to them.

'Gwen, look what the otters are doing!' shouted Flora.

'I know,' Gwen tried to call back.

'No, there!' Flora pointed ahead of her. Gwen looked and to her astonishment, she saw even more otters. They were scampering along the riverbank, dragging branches with them, diving into the river with the branches. They were building a barrier! If Gwen could just get close enough, she would be able to grab on to the dam and stop the water sweeping her away. She felt the otters around her guiding her towards it, their legs paddling hard.

The dam was getting closer and closer and as the tree branches loomed up, Gwen braced herself. She crashed into the dam, stopping her headlong rush through the water, and clung on to the wet wood. The otters swarmed around her, their bright eyes seeming to cheer her on.

Gwen gripped the branches and began

to haul herself out of the river as the otters squeaked encouragingly. The wood scratched her hands and arms and she panted with the effort, but little by little she pulled herself out on to the barrier and crawled along it to the riverbank.

Flora grabbed her as she half fell on to solid ground. 'Oh, Gwen. I thought you were going to die!'

'Me too,' said Gwen through chattering teeth. She felt exhausted.

Olivia came running down the path, her hair streaming behind her. 'Guinevere, are you all right?'

'Just about,' Gwen managed to gasp. 'I think now it's my turn to thank you for rescuing me!' She smiled. 'And your friends!'

'Otter friends, please help Guinevere warm up,' Olivia appealed.

The otters bounded over and surrounded Gwen, pressing themselves against her. Their bodies were wet too but warm. They snuggled around her, nuzzling her cold cheeks. As Gwen began to warm up, she started to laugh.

They were adorable with their twitching whiskers and sweet faces.

Flora crouched down and stroked them and they nuzzled her too.

Gradually Gwen stopped shivering and as she did so, she realised the river was calming down and the wind dropping. Morgana's magic must be wearing off. The clouds cleared and the sun came out, its rays helping to warm and dry her.

'I feel much better,' she said. Her hair was bedraggled and she knew she must look a state, but at least she wasn't shivering with cold any more.

'I'm so glad,' said Olivia, hugging her. 'Morgana must have set a spell on the bridge that was triggered by you releasing me.'

'We should get away from here before she

realises the wind and water haven't stopped us,' said Flora.

Gwen nodded. 'You should go back to Avalon, Olivia. Your sisters are waiting for you. You can use your magic and take yourself there, can't you?'

Olivia nodded. 'But what about you two?' she asked.

'We'll follow you to the Lake before we go home,' said Gwen. 'But don't worry, we won't be long. I think we might be able to find someone to help us.'

'Moonlight,' breathed Flora with a smile.

Moonlight was a beautiful white stallion that the girls had tamed. He lived in the woods and had helped them many times on their adventures when they needed to travel long distances or get to places quickly.

Gwen nodded. 'Go now,' she urged Olivia. 'Tell Nineve we'll join you soon.'

'Very well.' Olivia flashed a smile. 'Thank you again for rescuing me.' She turned to the watching otters. 'And thank you, my dear friends. Go back to your homes and may the magic of Avalon always keep you safe.'

She blew them a kiss and then clapped her hands. 'To Avalon!' she cried. There was flash of light, and by the time they blinked, Olivia had vanished.

Gwen and Flora stared at the place where she had been. Even though they had seen the other Spell Sisters do the same thing before, it was always breathtaking to see someone simply disappear in front of their eyes!

'Are you all right?' Flora took Gwen's hand.

Gwen squeezed her cousin's fingers.

'I'll be fine,' she said. 'So, shall we go and find Moonlight?'

'Oh, yes!' smiled Flora.

But as the girls hurried towards the trees, there was the sound of loud yapping. 'Look!' exclaimed Flora in dismay, as a white shape came hurtling towards them out of the trees. 'It's Louis!'

The dog ran over to them, but instead of attacking them he started jumping around them, licking them and putting his paws up on their knees to be patted. Flora blinked in astonishment as Gwen crouched down and ruffled his ears. 'What's happened to him?'

'Morgana's lost her power over animals now Olivia is free, remember?' said Gwen. 'Louis must have only been so bad-tempered because of Morgana's spells. I think it's why all the animals around here have been behaving strangely.

Now that the power over animals has returned to Olivia, Louis and all the other animals are back to normal.'

'Well, I like him much better like this,' said Flora, grinning. She bent down and Louis rolled on his back to have his tummy tickled.

'I suppose him being bad-tempered did help when he saw those rats,' said Gwen. 'I bet Morgana hadn't banked on us having a ratting dog with us!'

Flora laughed, and with Louis bounding at their feet, they ran into the woods.

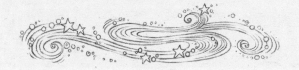

9

Return to Avalon

'Moonlight!' called Gwen. She put her fingers to her mouth and whistled. There was a pause and then a whinny rang out through the woodland and a beautiful stallion came cantering through the trees. His coat was as white as fresh snow and his mane and tail were long and silky. He gave a low pleased whicker as he saw the girls and came over to nuzzle them.

'We've already rescued the Spell Sister this time, boy,' Gwen told him. 'But will you take us to the Lake, please?'

Moonlight tossed his mane as if to say yes. Gwen helped Flora on.

'What about Louis?' Flora said.

Gwen saw the problem. They couldn't ride and carry the puppy. 'He'll have to run alongside us.'

'But Moonlight goes so fast,' Flora pointed out.

When Gwen had first met Moonlight, she had fed him an enchanted apple from Avalon, and since then he had been able to travel faster than any normal horse and seemed to understand what they said to him. Gwen hoped he could understand her now. 'Please go slowly this time, Moonlight,' she said, stroking his neck.

He nodded his head.

Gwen vaulted on. Holding on to Flora's waist, she touched her heels to Moonlight's sides and he trotted away with Louis running alongside him.

They soon reached the Lake and there in the centre of it was the enchanted island of Avalon, shrouded in purple mist. The Lake's still water shone like glass, but as Gwen dismounted and went over to the edge of it, she realised that the icy surface that Nineve had shown them in the pendant had melted away. 'It's not frozen any more!' she said with relief.

'That's right,' said a musical voice.

The water parted and Nineve, the Lady of the Lake, rose up through it, her long chestnut hair falling to her feet, her green and blue gown reaching to the surface of the water. Louis whined and sat down, staring at her.

Nineve smiled at Gwen and Flora. 'Thank you so much for rescuing Olivia. She is now back on Avalon, and she and her sisters helped me cast a spell to melt the ice. With all but one of them back on the island, the Spell Sisters' powers are growing strong again. They can't leave the island for fear of being trapped again, but now at least they are able to work together. And Morgana will not be able to stop me looking for Chloe the Storm Sister.'

'And when you find where she is, we'll go and free her!' declared Gwen. 'Then *all* of the Spell Sisters will be safe on Avalon again.'

'And Morgana's plan will have failed!' added Flora.

Nineve nodded. 'I hope so. But first Chloe has to be found and freed, and time is running out before the lunar eclipse. I shall begin looking for her as soon as possible. But first, I will take you to Avalon, so Olivia and her sisters can thank you themselves.'

She clapped her hands and instantly a white mist rose from the Lake and swirled round Gwen and Flora's feet. Flora quickly picked Louis up. Gwen grinned in delight as she felt the familiar sensation of floating, as the mist carried them out on to the Lake, and across its surface towards the island. Nineve ran ahead of them, and when they reached the centre of the Lake, the purple mist parted, revealing the island of Avalon. The girls followed Nineve, with Flora holding Louis tightly in her arms. He stared round at everything, his ears pricked.

As they stepped on to the island, Gwen smiled. It was such a different place now.

When they had first seen it, it had been dull and barren, the apple trees that covered it had bare branches and the streams had run dry. The house up a path had been empty and dark, but now the lights were on and it looked welcoming and cheerful. The island was green again, the apple trees heavy with ripening fruits. Insects buzzed around, birds sang, and for the first time Gwen spotted animals on Avalon too. Rabbits hopped across the grass, squirrels scampered around in the branches and shy deer peered out from behind tree trunks. Gwen even spotted two otters playing in a sparkling stream.

'Steady, boy,' soothed Flora as Louis struggled to get down, wanting to chase the squirrels and rabbits.

'Guinevere! Flora!' They heard Olivia's voice. She came running down the path to meet them, with her sisters following. They all hugged the girls and greeted them.

'Thank you so much for rescuing Olivia!' said Sophia the Flame Sister, her beautiful red hair shining in the sun. She had been the first Spell Sister the girls had freed.

'It's so wonderful to be home,' said Olivia happily. 'Thank you, girls. I really hope you can rescue our sister Chloe too.'

'We'll do our very best,' promised Gwen.

Sophia smiled. 'No one could do more.'

'Olivia told us about the trials you faced to free her,' said Lily the Forest Sister. 'We can't thank you enough!'

Olivia smiled at Gwen and Flora. 'I can see my sisters have all given you gemstones. It's my turn now,' she said, looking at the six gems already hanging on the silver necklace around

Gwen's neck. She cupped her hands together and whispered a few words. A light seemed to glow inside her closed fingers. Very slowly she opened them up and revealed a tiny white mouse sitting on her palms. In his front paws he was holding a glowing red ruby, the same colour as his bright eyes. Gwen and Flora gasped.

Olivia walked over and held up the mouse to Gwen's necklace. He placed the stone beside the others and, with a red flash, it attached itself to the silver chain. With a happy squeak, the mouse scampered up Olivia's arm and perched on her shoulder, peering out from her dark hair, his whiskers twitching.

'Thank you,' breathed Gwen.

'It is my pleasure. I hope it will come in very useful one day soon. Thank you both again for rescuing me,' said Olivia, taking their hands, her eyes glowing as she smiled at them.

'It is time for you to go now, girls,' called Nineve. She'd been watching from the water.

Gwen and Flora hugged all the Spell Sisters, and then with a chorus of goodbyes and thank yous ringing in their ears, they ran down to join Nineve.

'One more freed,' Nineve said with a warm smile, as she looked at the seven Spell Sisters who were all gathered together, waving.

Gwen nodded. 'And one still to go.'

Nineve took the girls back across the Lake

and then they mounted Moonlight and said goodbye.

'I shall be in touch very soon,' promised Nineve. 'We've come so far, and with only a few days until the lunar eclipse, we must not let Morgana take Avalon now. Keep the pendant with you at all times so I can contact you.'

'I will,' promised Gwen.

'Goodbye, Nineve,' said Flora, placing Louis on the ground. 'We'll see you soon!'

'Goodbye, my friends!' called Nineve, waving from the water, as Moonlight cantered away with the small dog bounding along beside him.

✦ ✦ ✦

'Oh dear, I hope Mother hasn't been looking for us,' Flora said anxiously, after they had left Moonlight in the woods and were walking back

up the hill towards the castle. The sun was starting
to sink in the sky. Louis ran alongside them, his
tail wagging, his tongue hanging out as he panted.
His once white coat was now a dirty brown from
the mud by the riverbank and he had brambles
and twigs caught in his fluffy fur, but he looked
very happy.

Gwen's clothes had dried after her dip in

the river. She was very glad her dress and cloak were a dark green and didn't show the dirt. 'Let's sneak in,' she said. 'And then we can pretend we've been back in the castle for ages if Aunt Matilda comes looking for us.'

Flora nodded. But their plan failed as they tiptoed up the staircase towards their bedchamber. The heavy oak door that led into the Great Hall opened and Aunt Matilda sailed out. She stopped abruptly when she saw them. 'Guinevere! Flora! Have you been out all this time?'

She stared at them, waiting for a response.

'Sorry, Mother. We thought we'd take Louis for a really long walk to see if it helped his mood,' Flora began. 'And. . .'

'Louis!' Aunt Matilda's hand flew to her chest as her gaze fell on the muddy dog. 'What a state he's in! Where have you been with him?'

Louis looked round at the sound of his name. Seeing Lady Matilda, he gave a friendly bark and trotted over. He wagged his tail and panted.

Lady Matilda stared. 'What's happened to him?'

Louis pawed at her foot and whined, asking to be stroked.

'He's. . . he's being friendly!' Lady Matilda stammered.

'Yes, the walk seemed to do him good,' Gwen said quickly. 'I think he just needed to run off some energy.'

Lady Matilda reached down and cautiously stroked Louis's head. The little dog licked her and then rolled over on his back.

'Goodness me!' said Lady Matilda, looking as if she couldn't believe her eyes. 'He's like a different dog!'

She tickled Louis's tummy and he wriggled with delight. A fond smile spread over Lady Matilda's face. 'Well, this is a big improvement. He may be looking rather muddy, but you've done a wonderful job with him, girls. Thank you.'

Flora and Gwen breathed sighs of relief. Lady Matilda scooped Louis up. 'I shall go and find someone to give him a bath.' She looked down at the little dog. 'You'd like to be clean and fluffy again, wouldn't you, little one?' she cooed. Louis licked her nose and Lady Matilda smiled happily before hurrying away.

The breath left Gwen in a rush. 'Thank goodness. She was so caught up by Louis that she didn't even notice my clothes!'

'I'm very glad Louis is friendly again,' said Flora.

'And it's all thanks to Olivia being freed,' said Gwen. 'Now, we just have to rescue Chloe.' She looked out of the window on the staircase. The sky was blue, but dark storm clouds hovered on the horizon. 'We must free her from wherever Morgana has trapped her.'

'We will.' Flora squeezed her hand. 'And as soon as she's back on Avalon, the island will be safe from Morgana for good.'

Their eyes met. Gwen thought about the beautiful island and the seven Spell Sisters all waiting for their final sister to return. 'Nothing will stop us,' she declared bravely. 'Absolutely nothing at all!'

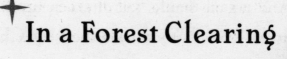

In a Forest Clearing

Deep in the forest, a long scream rang out. Morgana Le Fay swept around a clearing in front of a massive oak tree – the entrance to her lair. 'No!' she shrieked. 'I cannot believe those girls have thwarted me again. My magic should have been able to stop them. How did they rescue that wretched Spell Sister? How?'

A squirrel was watching from a nearby

branch. Morgana sent a ball of green fire flying straight at him. With an alarmed squeak, he leaped from the branch and sped away, and the ball of fire hit the tree trunk and exploded into green sparks. 'Stupid animal!' Morgana shrieked.

A baby deer was peeping round a tree. Morgana shot fire at him too. He leaped back and bounded away, his white tail bobbing.

Morgana watched the sparks fly into the sky. 'Those girls will pay for this,' she muttered.

Her eyes narrowed as she thought deeply. 'They will not rescue the final Spell Sister. There are only two weeks until the lunar eclipse, and while she remains trapped I will still be able to claim Avalon and its power. It only takes one captured sister for my plan to succeed. I shall use all my power against those interfering girls. They will not defeat me. I will not allow it.' Her eyes glittered like dark jewels. 'Avalon shall be mine!'

And shooting another burst of green fire defiantly into the air, she turned and stalked furiously into her lair. Overhead, the storm clouds crept further across the sky.

Turn over for a sneak peek of
the next SPELL SISTERS adventure!

CHLOE
THE STORM SISTER

Spell Sisters

It was cold inside the little chapel as they stood and listened to Bethany and Guy practise saying their vows. Gwen was already starting to feel a bit bored as she stood behind Bethany, and she glanced around idly at the decorative windows of the little church. Most of the stained glass panes were old and dusty, so she couldn't really see through them out to the woods. Wishing she could be outside again, Gwen watched little circles of sunlight dancing on the floor, shining in through what seemed to be a newer, cleaner window. As Gwen watched the

spots of light, she thought about Avalon and the
way the light danced on the Lake around it.

Where could the last Spell Sister be trapped,
and what exactly were her powers? Each of the
sisters of Avalon had a magical power that related
to nature and elements and Nineve had told them
that the eighth sister was Chloe the Storm Sister,

so Gwen guessed that must mean she had power over the weather. Morgana had been able to use

the magic of each of the Spell Sisters while they were trapped and with all the other sisters now safe, the only power Morgana could use, apart from her own magic, would be Chloe's. *I really hope we find Chloe in time*, Gwen thought anxiously, she didn't like to think what would happen if they failed.

At long last the rehearsal came to an end. 'Well done everyone, our practise is done,' announced Thomas. 'You may all now return to the castle. I'll see you all tomorrow for the happy event!' he finished with a smile.

Gwen breathed a sigh of relief. With the rehearsal over everything was ready for the wedding. Maybe now she and Flora could finally slip away.

'Gwen? What's that?' She looked round to see Arthur staring at her dress. Gwen glanced down to follow his gaze and gave a squeak of alarm. The blue pendant, tucked inside the neck of her dress, was glowing!

Arthur blinked at the shining light. 'What. . . what is it?'

'Nothing!' Gwen hastily pulled her cloak around herself, hiding the light. 'Nothing at all!'

'But there's something shining around your neck. . .'

Explanations tumbled through Gwen's head, but she knew Arthur was too clever to be fobbed off with a lie. There was only one thing for it – to tell him the truth. Or at least a little bit of it.

'Please, Arthur,' she begged quietly, checking to see no one else was listening. 'Don't say anything to anyone. You're right, my necklace is glowing.'

'Is it. . . *magic*?' he whispered in awe.

She hesitated for a moment, and then nodded. 'I wish I could tell you all about it, I really do but I can't. I've promised not to tell a soul. Flora is the only other person who knows what's going on.'

His eyes met hers. 'All right,' he sighed. 'If it's a secret I won't ask any more. You mustn't break a promise.'

Gwen could have hugged him. 'Thank you!' she said, reaching over to squeeze Arthur's arm gratefully. 'Now, I need to talk to Flora, but we can't have anyone else notice us slip away. . .'

Gwen glanced over at Flora, who was standing with the pages by the chapel door.

'I'll distract the others for you,' said Arthur.

Gwen grinned widely. 'That would be really helpful, thanks.'

Arthur strode to the door. 'Hey, who wants a wrestling contest? Bet I can beat the lot of you with one hand tied behind my back!'

There was an immediate outcry from the other pages.

'No you can't—!'

'You're talking a load of pigswill—'

'You'll certainly never beat me!' Will interrupted with a sneer.

'Well, I suppose there's only one way to find out,' said Arthur. 'Race you to the keep!' He set off and, fired up by the challenge, the other pages chased after him like a pack of hounds hunting a hare.

'So,' Flora came over to her, her eyebrows

raised. 'You and Arthur looked like you were having a cosy chat?'

'Flora, there isn't time for this now!' Gwen whispered. 'The pendant's glowing!'

The teasing look dropped instantly from Flora's face. 'Glowing? That means Nineve must be sending us a message!'

Gwen nodded. 'We need to find somewhere private so we can find out what she's needs to tell us.'

She darted out of the chapel with Flora following. The pages had disappeared back towards the castle, and only a few adults remained, talking as they made their way back as well. 'This way,' said Gwen, quickly leading the way into the trees near the chapel.

They hid behind the wide trunk of a horse chestnut tree and Gwen pulled out the necklace.

As well as the blue pendant, seven gems hung on the silver chain. Each one had been given to Gwen by a different sister of Avalon to say thank for rescuing her. There was a fire agate stone from Sophia, an emerald from Lily, a piece of amber from Isabella, a purple amethyst from Amelia, a sapphire from Grace, a ruby from Olivia and a pearl from Evie. The blue pendant Gwen had originally pulled from the stone by the Lake was larger than all of them. It was now sparkling with light.

'Nineve?' Gwen whispered, picking it up.

A mist swirled across the pendant's surface and an image of the Lady of the Lake appeared. She had dark eyes and long chestnut hair, and wore a shimmering green and blue dress that fell to her ankles. A circle of pearls held back her thick hair from her beautiful face. 'Guinevere!

Flora!' she said. 'You must come to the Lake with all speed!'

'Now?' Gwen said.

'Yes. I have finally found out where Chloe, the eighth sister, is trapped.'

Gwen and Flora exchanged excited looks.

'You must rescue her before tonight,' Nineve went on, her eyes full of intent. 'My protection spell will fade as soon as the lunar eclipse starts. As the Earth, moon and sun move into line, a shadow will cross the moon and when it falls completely dark, the spell will break and Morgana will be able to cross the Lake and reach Avalon.' Nineve hesitated, and her voice wavered a little. 'Once she is there, nothing will stop her from using its power to bring chaos to the kingdom. Our only chance is to free Chloe the Storm Sister so she can join with her sisters on Avalon. Together, the eight Spell Sisters have enough power to keep her from reaching the island.'

'We'll come to the Lake straight away,' Gwen said.

'Thank you, girls. I will see you soon,' Nineve said.

The image in the pendant faded.

'The last Spell Sister, finally,' said Flora. She looked excited but nervous. 'I wonder where she's trapped?'

'I don't know,' Gwen said anxiously. 'We need to find Moonlight. He'll be able to take us to the Lake as quickly as possible. There's no time to lose.' She walked further into the trees and whistled softly. Moonlight was a wild white stallion. The girls had found him in the woods on their first adventure, and Gwen had fed him an apple from Avalon. After eating it, he had

developed magical powers – he could gallop at incredible speed, and seemed able to understand the girls. He lived in the woods, but Moonlight was always there for them when they needed him.

Gwen listened for a moment, and then whistled again. This time, while the sound of Gwen's summons was still echoing through the trees, there was the soft thud of hoofbeats, and then Moonlight came trotting through the trees. His ears were pricked and his neck arched proudly. His mane and tail hung in soft silky strands and his coat was the colour of freshly fallen snow.

Gwen's heart leapt as it always did when she saw him. She smiled, and hugged his neck quickly. 'We need to go to the Lake, Moonlight. Please can you take us there?'

The stallion whickered and walked over to a fallen tree trunk. He stood there patiently, as if telling the girls to use it to get on his back. Gwen helped Flora on and then vaulted up behind her cousin. The stallion's back was warm and soft.

Flora wrapped her hands in his mane. 'Oh please, Moonlight,' she breathed. 'Take us to the Lake as fast as you can.'

Will Gwen and Flora be able to rescue Chloe?

Read the rest of

CHLOE

THE STORM SISTER

to find out!

MAKE A FUN ANIMAL MASK!

Create some animal magic of your own
by following the simple steps below and
creating a unique animal mask.

What you'll need:

+ A paper plate
+ Paint/crayons/felt-tip pens
+ Glue, tape or a stapler
+ Plain card or paper
+ Paintbrush

+ An ice-lolly stick
+ Scissors

*Remember to
always be careful when
you're working with scissors and
glue or ask a grown-up
to help you.*

TOP TIPS

+ *Be as creative as you like
with the animal you choose!
You can be anything from a snake
to a sea lion, a rabbit to a raccoon!*

+ *Why not get your friends to
make masks too and then put
on an animal show!*

HOW TO MAKE YOUR MASK:

1. First decide what animal you're going to be – maybe a dog or a cat or even an otter! Then paint or colour-in your paper plate the right colour for your animal using your paint/crayons.

2. Wait until your plate is dry, then cut out two eye hole about a third of the way down the plate.

3. Paint or draw a nose in the centre of the plate. Again think about what animal you're trying to be and make sure the nose matches!

4. Cut the card or paper into the shape of a tongue and then colour it in pink. Draw a smiley black mouth beneath the nose and glue the tongue into the centre of the mouth.

5. Cut more card or paper into ears – if you're a cat make them pointed, if you're a dog make them round. Glue the ears to the top of the paper plate with one each side.

6. Glue an ice-lolly stick to the bottom of the plate for your handle.

VISIT WWW.SPELLSISTERS.CO.UK AND

Plus lots of other enchanted extras!

Spell Sisters news

Explore Avalon

More about Gwen and Flora's quest

Spell Sister profiles

Activity sheets

Wallpapers

Your chance to get in touch with us

ENTER THE MAGICAL WORLD OF AVALON!

Spell Sisters